OUR BUILDING

For the children past, present,
and future living in Buildings
everywhere. May you always be
inspired by the heights of your
homes, that reveal endless horizons.
~J.C.

For Fran
~R.J.

OUR BUILDING

JOSEPH COELHO   RICHARD JOHNSON

Frances Lincoln
Children's Books

Our Building is gray.

Concrete and gray.

Boring, hard, and gray.

But Our Building is high,
so very high.
From its fabled height,
we can see rushing waves of green
beyond the gray of the block,

beyond the black of the roads,
beyond the aches of our legs.

From the window of Our Building,
we see a tree gazing up at us
with big leafy brows.

It sings in rustles and whooshes.
Rustles and whooshes
that only we hear.
That the passers by
down below
cannot hear.
Have forgotten how to hear.

But we do,
and the song vibrates within us.

Down the steps we creep,
past the elevators and garbage chutes
and the bags of trash and door mats,
away from the overheard coughs and barks,
away from the satellite dishes.
We creep away from Our Building.

Past the cars on the streets
and the flickering street lights,
to the fields and forests
that border our apartment block.

The tree that we see
from atop Our Building
is in a forest,
but which tree?
Which tree
is the tree with bushy brows
singing the song of rustles and whooshes?

The bark of the first tree
is smooth to the touch,
too smooth to be an old singer.

The bark of the second tree
is sappy and wet,
too sad to gaze at the Building.

But the bark of the third tree is old ...

... old and wrinkled,
warm and cracked,
and from a crack a song is spilling,
a song of rustles and whooshes.

The crack widens
and the song sucks
and the trunk is deep
and we tumble in.

At the bottom of the tree
is a world that is secret that Our Building never sees.
That the elevators have never groaned for,
where concrete steps have never been,
a world deeper than anything Our Building has ever seen.

There are creatures lurking
between the rocks on the ground.
There are things making ear-aching noises
that sing with a hacking, coughing sound.

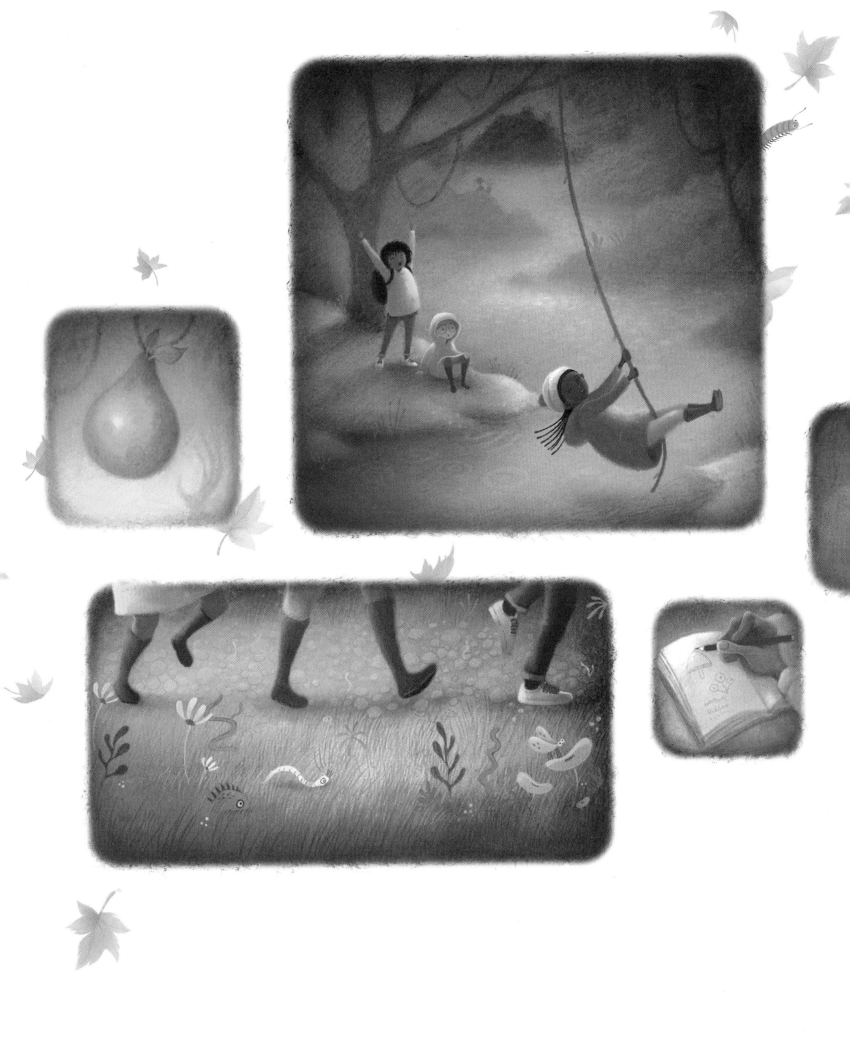

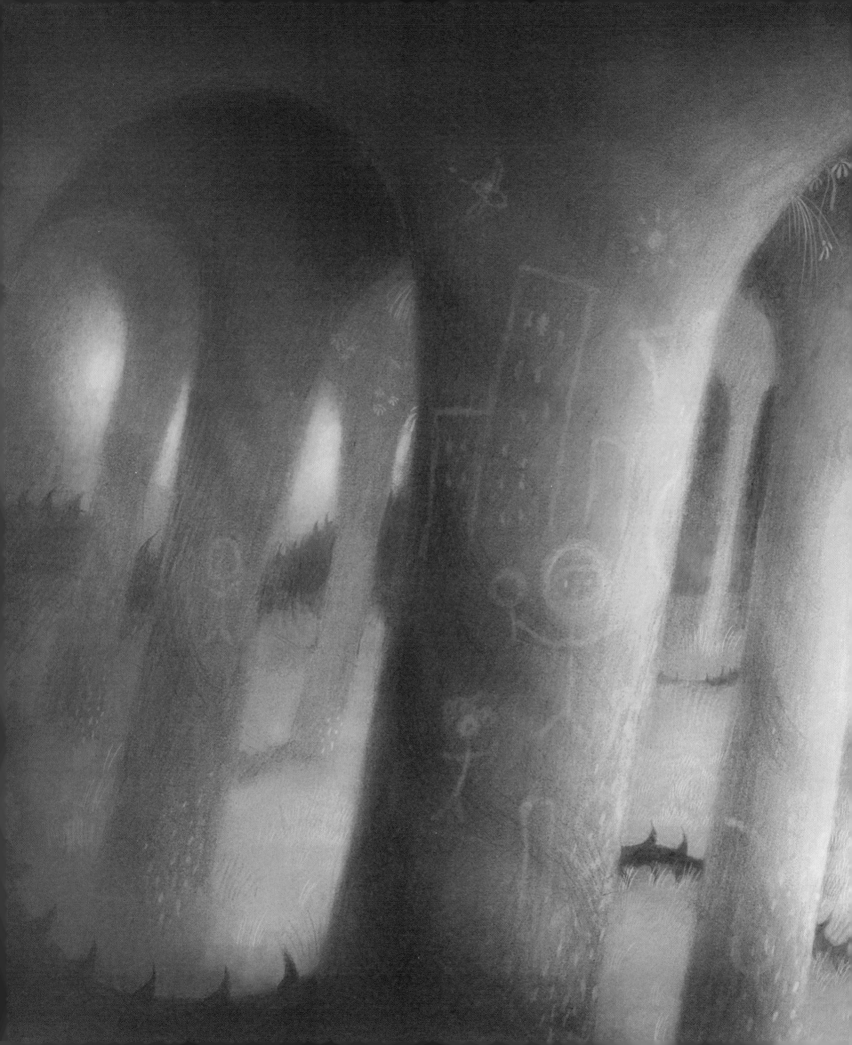

There are figures that flit like shadows
painted across the earthen walls.
There are thundering snarling beasts
forever chasing balls.

And when you turn into the chamber
of the mushroom glowing night,
there are gleaming metallic visions that soar,
zigzag, and take flight.

And on the spiky tendrils
of the most labyrinthine roots,
you can taste the sweet deliciousness
of the steaming dessert fruits.

Sitting in a wooden hug
of an old and tree-grown throne
is a wizened, tree-grown man
with bushy brows and a gaze that is well known.

He saw the Buildings rise
with cranes and concrete.
He saw the elevators lift
the people up from the street.

He saw us wander and creep
from Our Building way up high,
and he has ...

... a stone for us!

A stone for us!

A stone for us!

A stone so smooth and ordinary
but with a hole right through its middle,
and when we peer through it,
the world goes upside-a-diddle.

The things that are fantastic
in the world beneath Our Building
now look terribly ordinary,
just roots and mushrooms and flowers.

But as we rise up the trunk
that is both so high and so deep
and climb out from the tree cracks
that sing and whoosh and weep ...

... we gaze upon Our Building,
towering up above
and through the stone-hole
see the Building has eyes ...

... eyes that are full of love.

We see the concrete brows
that the balconies now make.
We see the elevator mouth
that laughs as it shakes.

And as the stone guides us
to the magic of Our Building,
we see the wondrous creatures
that dance on each doormat.

There are critters that sparkle
as if composed of glass.
There are voices in puffs of smoke
that whisper secrets and intrigue and laugh.

And as we touch our fingertips to
the concrete pillars that anchor our block,
we feel a song spill from them
that connects our homes to the land's bedrock.

And the adults don't remember
the wonder of Our Building,
or that a hole in a stone can reveal how
the humdrum can hide a flower.

The adults knew, but then forgot
the wonder of the tree-grown throne,
but you'll remind them of the secret
of a power that is home-grown.

A power that resides
in the smiles of our neighbors.
A magic that seeps out
when we swap our home-baked flavors.

An enchantment that sparkles
from the holding open of the elevator-door.
A gratitude that radiates
when two carry groceries to a front door.

A power that is ours
that lives deep within our bones.
A power that connects us all
to an ancient tree-grown throne.

And then we'll all see
the beauty of Our Building,
and together we'll all remember
our own, deep hidden power.

Our Building © 2024 Quarto Publishing plc.
Text © 2022 Joseph Coelho • Illustrations © 2022 Richard Johnson

First published in the US in 2024 by Frances Lincoln Children's, an imprint of The Quarto Group.
100 Cummings Center, Suite 265D, Beverly, MA 01915, USA.
T +1 978-282-9590 F +1 078-283-2742 www.Quarto.com

A CIP record for this book is available from the Library of Congress.
ISBN 978-0-7112-6884-5
eISBN 978-0-7112-6883-8

The illustrations were created using gouache paints.
Set in Adobe Garamond

Published by Peter Marley
Designed by Myrto Dimitrakoulia
Commissioned and edited by Lucy Brownridge
Production by Dawn Cameron

Manufactured in Guangdong, China TT042024
1 3 5 7 9 8 6 4 2

MIX
Paper | Supporting
responsible forestry
FSC
www.fsc.org
FSC® C016973